LANA's WORLD
LET'S HAVE A PARADE!

To Morgan, Leilani, and baby Ellen, with love
—E.S.

For Jordan
—J.G.

Text copyright © 2015 by Erica Silverman
Illustrations copyright © 2015 by Jess Golden

For information about permission to reproduce selections from this book,
write to Permissions, Houghton Mifflin Harcourt Publishing Company,
215 Park Avenue South, New York, New York 10003.

www.hmhco.com

The text of this book is set in Caecelia LT Std.
The display type was set in Gil Sans.
The illustrations were made with watercolors, pastels, and colored pencils.

Library of Congress Cataloging-in-Publication Data
Silverman, Erica.
Lana's world: let's have a parade / Erica Silverman.
p. cm. — (Lana's world) (Green light readers. Level 2)
Summary: Unable to interest her parents, her brothers, or even her dog in
having a parade in the rain, Lana lines up her toys in the hallway and is
soon leading the parade of her dreams.
ISBN 978-0-544-10677-2 paper over board
ISBN 978-0-544-10678-9 trade paper
[1. Parades—Fiction. 2. Family life—Fiction. 3. Imagination—Fiction. 4. Rain
and rainfall—Fiction.] I. Title.
PZ7.S58625Leu 2014
[E]—dc23
2013004557

Manufactured in China
SCP 10 9 8 7 6 5 4 3 2 1

4500520603

LANA's WORLD

LET'S HAVE A PARADE!

Written by **Erica Silverman**
Illustrated by **Jess Golden**

GREEN LIGHT READERS
HOUGHTON MIFFLIN HARCOURT
BOSTON NEW YORK

Pitter pitter pat, sang the rain.

Mama was making pancakes.

"Let's have a parade," said Lana.

"It's raining," said Mama.

Papa set the table.

"Let's have a parade," said Lana.

"We'll all get wet," said Papa.

Jay poured syrup.
So did Ray.
"Let's have a parade," said Lana.

"Who wants to get wet?" said Jay.
"Not me!" said Ray.

Furry munched on a pancake.
"Let's have a parade," said Lana.

"Woof!" Furry curled up in his bed.

"I will have a parade by myself," said Lana.

In the hallway, she lined up
a horse, a bear, a clown on skates,
and a mouse on a bike.

She put a queen in a wagon.
"This is your float," she said.
She picked up her drum.

"Now . . . let's have a parade,"
whispered Lana.

The hall became a street.
Cheering crowds lined the sidewalk.
Banners flapped in the wind.
Lana raised her drumstick.

Rat-a-tat-tat!

Dum-da-da-dum!

Sis-boom-ba!

Pitter pitter pat, sang the rain.

"May I join your parade?" asked Mama.
"I have bells."
"Join in," said Lana.

Rat-a-tat-tat!

Dum-da-da-dum!

Sis-boom-ba!

Ting-a-ling-ling!

Pitter pitter pat, sang the rain.

"May I join your parade?" asked Papa.

"I have a train whistle."

"Join in," said Lana.

Rat-a-tat-tat!
Dum-da-da-dum!
Sis-boom-ba!
Ting-a-ling-ling!
Whoo whoo!
Pitter pitter pat, sang the rain.

"May I join your parade?" asked Jay.

"Me too?" asked Ray.

"We brought cymbals," said Jay.

"They're loud!" said Ray.

"Join in," said Lana.

Rat-a-tat tat!
Dum-da-da-dum!
Sis-boom-ba!
Ting-a-ling-ling!
Whoo whoo!
Cling cling clang!
Pitter pitter pat,
sang the rain.

"Woof!" barked Furry.

"Join in, Furry," said Lana.

"You can sing."

Lana looked around.

"Is everybody ready?"

"Yes! Yes! Yes!" they all shouted.

"Let's have a parade!"

The horse pranced.

The bear danced.

The clown skated.

The queen waved.

Rat-a-tat-tat!
Dum-da-da-dum!
Sis-boom-ba!
Ting-a-ling-ling!
Whoo whoo!
Cling cling clang!
"Woooooof!"
Pitter pitter pat,
sang the rain.

The parade marched up one street
and down another.
Crowds cheered.
Banners flapped.

"Marching in the rain
is fun," said Mama.

"Making music in the
rain is fun," said Papa.

"Marching in puddles
is fun," said Jay.
"Splash!" said Ray.

Furry shook, shook, shook.
Water sprayed everywhere.
"Oh, Furry!" they all said.

"A rainy-day parade is the best
parade of all!" said Lana.
And then they marched on . . .
all the way home.

Rat-a-tat-tat!

Dum-da-da-dum!

Sis-boom-ba!

Ting-a-ling-ling!

Whoo whoo!

Cling cling clang!

"Wooooof!"

Pitter pitter pat, sang the rain.